MARGRET & H.A.RE

Curious George

Makes Pancakes

Illustrated in the style of H. A. Rey by Vipah Interactive

Houghton Mifflin Harcourt
Boston New York

Copyright © 1998 by Houghton Mifflin Harcourt Publishing Company

Based on the character of Curious George®, created by Margret and H. A. Rey.
Illustrated by Vipah Interactive, Wellesley, Massachusetts: C. Becker, D. Fakkel, M. Jensen,
S. SanGiacomo, C. Witte, C. Yu.

The text of this book is set in 17-pt. Adobe Garamond.
The illustrations are watercolor and charcoal pencil, reproduced in full color.

www.hmhco.com

Library of Congress Cataloging-in-Publication Data

Curious George makes pancakes / based on the original character by Margret and H. A. Rey.
p. cm.
Summary: Curious George, an inquisitive monkey, causes quite a stir when he tries his
"hand" at making pancakes at a fundraiser for the children's hospital.

ISBN: 978-0-547-49916-1

[1. Monkeys—Fiction. 2. Pancakes, waffles, etc.—Fiction. 3. Fundraising—Fiction.]
I. Rey, Margret, 1906–1996. II. Rey, H. A. (Hans Augusto), 1898–1977.
PZ7.C921643   1998
[E]—dc21   98-12350 CIP AC

Manufactured in China
LEO 12
4500682011

This is George.

George was a good little monkey and always very curious.

One morning the man with the yellow hat woke George early.

"Time to get up, George," he said. "The pancake breakfast is today."

George loved the pancake breakfast. It was a fundraiser held every year to make money for special programs at the children's hospital.

Besides eating pancakes, there were all kinds of games to play. Even the mayor came to play and eat, but first he gave a welcome speech.

"Thank you all for coming," the mayor said. "We appreciate your generous support."

He thanked all the volunteers who were helping that day and finally he said, "Please enjoy yourselves . . .

and the pancakes!"

When the mayor finished, the man with the yellow hat said, "George, I'm going to buy our tickets. Please wait here and don't be too curious."

George waited like a good little monkey, but — *mmm!* — something smelled good!

Could it be the pancakes?
George was curious.

He followed the delicious
smell and found a whole griddle
full of pancakes! George watched
as a man poured little batter
circles and flipped them up in
the air.

It looked like fun
to make pancakes!

George wanted to help.

On a table near the griddle was a basket full of blueberries.

These pancakes need blueberries, George thought. And he sprinkled some on top.

Meanwhile, the man
at the griddle was so busy
he didn't notice the little monkey
helping him. But the line grew and grew...

George's pancakes were a hit! Soon everyone wanted them and the man could not keep up. "Please wait," he said to someone holding an empty plate. "I need to find an assistant to help me." And just like that, he was gone.

George looked at the people waiting in line and then at the empty griddle. Why, he could make pancakes. He could be the assistant!

George poured the batter into nice round circles.

Next he added blueberries.

He waited just a minute to let the pancakes cook.

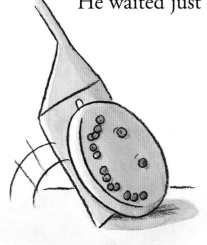

Then he flipped them over.

And last, he added syrup.

The line for pancakes was enormous. But with four hands, George made quite a chef—and no one's plate was empty for long.

"I've been coming to this breakfast for years," a man said. "But I've never seen pancakes made like this before!"

"I've never eaten this many pancakes before," said a girl.

"I didn't even like pancakes before!" said another girl. And they all lined up for more.

When the man returned with his new assistant, he was shocked to see a monkey making pancakes. "This is no place for a monkey!" he yelled, and he began to chase George.

George hadn't meant to cause trouble. He'd only wanted to help. Now he only wanted to get away. Quickly, George found a place to hide, and the man and his assistant ran right by.

But where did George go?

When it was safe to come out, George jumped down. He was covered in syrup like a pancake — and he was sticking to everything! George was curious: could these napkins help him get clean?

No! The napkins only made it worse.

What George needed was some water to wash with ... why, here was the perfect thing.

George climbed up.

This would do the trick for a sticky monkey!

George sat on the bench and splashed himself with water. But all of a sudden...

Splash! George was IN the water. What a surprise! George climbed up again and splashed back down. He'd never been in a dunk tank before, and he'd never had so much fun getting clean! Soon everyone

was having fun, and the line at the dunk tank grew even longer than the line for pancakes. Later, the mayor came by. "I've heard all about your delicious pancakes," he said. "You've made our fundraiser a big success and I have a special favor to ask you..."

At the end of the day, George got to present the money from the fundraiser to the president of the hospital. "Thanks to you, George, this has been our best year ever!" she said. "Will you come back and make pancakes again next year?"

George nodded and everyone cheered.